Snipers Among Us

By David G Evans

TABLE OF CONTENTS

SNIPERS AMONG US

Plot

Earth was overpopulated and contaminated in 2154. While the wealthy reside on Corysum, an orbiting space station, the majority of the population lives in poverty.

In an effort to smuggle people into using their Med-Bays, which can treat any ailment or condition, a hacker by the name of Spider operates flights to Corysum. However, these flights are frequently shot down.

When Max Da Costa unintentionally receives a fatal dose of radiation, he's employed as a laborer by Armadyne Corp.

He's given medicine and informed that he has five days left before losing his job. In order to get a trip to Corysum in exchange for Max stealing information for Spider, Max, and his companion Julio approach Spider.

Defense Secretary Delacourt of Corysum fires down multiple spacecraft as they approach the torus and receives criticism from the President.

Delacourt, upset, contacts John Carlyle, CEO of Armadyne Corp, and offers him life-long defense contracts in exchange for a program that will enable Delacourt to stage a coup and become President.

The program is created by Carlyle, who then stores it in his head. Carlyle is chosen by Max and Julio to be the source of information theft and have his shuttle to Corysum shot down.

They rob Carlyle of the program, which forces Delacourt to dispatch a black ops team led by Kruger to recover it.

While killing Julio and Spider's entire crew, Kruger leaves an injured Max to flee with the information. Frey, a nurse, and Max's childhood friend, offers to help.

He’s patched up by her, and he flees before Kruger can find him. Spider, who Max visits, recognizes the value of the information in Max's thoughts.

Up till Corysum, all flights are grounded by Delacourt. Preventing Max from being taken by Spider.

While Max approaches Kruger and offers him the information in exchange for the use of a Med-Bay, Kruger finds Frey and abducts her together with her daughter.

The lockdown is lifted once Kruger accepts, allowing them to leave for Corysum. During the flight, Kruger and Max fight over the data and a grenade explodes in Kruger's face killing him.

The ship crashes and Max is arrested and taken to Delacourt, who orders a team to extract the data even if it kills Max.

Max escapes and heads to the armory to save Frey, who has been turned over to Kruger's men. Kruger is revived on a Med-Bay and confronted by Delacourt, whom he fatally wounds.

He orders his men to start killing the politicians on the station while he hunts down Max. Spider discovers Max after successfully landing on Corysum.

He strikes a deal with Max in which, in return for the information, his men will protect Frey and deliver her daughter to a Med-Bay.

They proceed to the center of the computer, where Kruger meets them. Max and Kruger battle viciously until Max throws a grenade at Kruger, killing him.

As soon as Max and Spider are connected to the computer, Spider recognizes that if Max downloads the data, it will kill him.

As he bids Frey farewell and starts the download, Max kills himself but leaves Frey free to heal her daughter.

Chapter 1

*****

PREQUEL

In Portland, Oregon, it was a stormy night. The entire day had been clouded in rain and oppressive thunderstorms.

All through the night, the town was pounded by angry showers. Small tree branches, leaves, and loose trash were blown across the street by strong winds.

Matthew Ziegler, a biochemist, was working in his lab on this late, rainy night when most families would be huddled together in front of their stoves and fires, enjoying movies, meals, and stories.

Matthew has always wanted to be a part of a significant endeavor that has the potential to alter the course of history.

Now that he had this wonderful opportunity, he gladly set aside his family and his daughter in order to give it his full attention.

It didn't matter to him that it meant giving up his family and social life. At this point, nothing was more important to him. Anything would have been worth it to him to get this chance.

His collaborator on the project was microbiologist Lucy Dawson. She was the one person he could rely on to help him with such a task.

Despite the fact that she was well known for her abilities, she was currently greatly annoyed by his narrow focus. "Sir, I think we need to call it a day," Lucy told Matthew.

Her almond shaped eyes glistened from the partially dark room as she looked at him. Worry and irritation laced her voice, because all she wanted right then was to be tucked away in her warm, cozy bed, curled up next to her husband. But Dr. Matthew hadn't even noticed she was talking to him because he was so preoccupied with his work.

He was completely absorbed in what he was doing, so while he was aware that she was speaking.

He was unable to understand what she was saying. After he finished the project, the only thing he hoped to hear was the word "Eureka."

She yelled, "Sir! once again.

Lucy, not now. I'm nearly done. We're going to make history, Dr. Martin exclaimed with a broad grin on his face. "Pick up your gloves and assist me in holding this vial.

This ZHF virus is the original, we can finish up after I simply add a little brain tissue. You can visit your hubby at home.

He handed her the flask with a flat bottom and urged, "Hurry up. The moment he tried to add some brain tissue to the vial of ZHF after taking some out of the freezer, the storm cut off the electricity, plunging the entire lab into darkness.

He stumbled back in shock and yelled, "Dammit!" Why did this need to occur at this time?

The lightening crackled lighting up the chamber for a brief minute before sinking them back into an inky dark world. Dr. Matthew snarled with frustration, "Let's hope the backup generator turns on soon."

A small bit of the substance in the vial had spilled on Lucy's hand as the lights went out and the lab was immediately enveloped in darkness.

She gave herself a mental pat on the back for having the good judgment to put on her lab coat and gloves.

"I must go do the dishes. I'm fatigued and it's already late, and this outage doesn't help.

Tomorrow, we may continue this "Lucy muttered angrily.

But Lucy, Dr. Matthew tried to stop Lucy, but by the time she did. She had put the experiment back on the table and had already left the room without even turning around.

As she walked away, he let out a loud sigh, and the backup generator started as if by magic. Matthew decided it would be better to carry on with the project at this point, even if it meant working by himself.

Lucy arrived at the restroom in the lab. She had a lot of frustration. She wouldn't have consented to take part in this research.

If it weren't for the fact that she needed the funding that the government was willing to provide for it or the opportunity to collaborate with someone as smart as Dr. Matthew.

She wouldn't have consented to take part in this endeavor. Thank God, she and Dr. Matthew only contributed to the biological component of the weapon, despite the fact that it was extremely harmful and even life-threatening. The dreaded job would be done by the engineers in Miami.

After this, she was finished as for herself! As Lucy travelled the winding path back to her house, her eyes started to fog over. Because of the highly sensitive nature of the work, she and Dr. Matthew was doing, it was mandated by federal legislation that their facility be at least five miles away from any densely populated regions.

He was a clever man, he has successfully developed several treatments for many of the most debilitating diseases in the world, including Ebola, Alzheimer's, and he even made a vain attempt to work on the AIDS virus.

As Lucy handled the driving wheel around the dark, rainy streets, she became aware of an itch all over her hands and wrist and started to scratch it.

Now, the city lights were starting to turn back on. She had promised her husband, Matt, a romantic evening.

Her favorite dark chocolate, dinner, and a glass of red wine. She at least hoped it would be passionate.

Her body temperature had steadily started to increase since she had left the lab, and an intense headache had abruptly struck her, making her unable to concentrate on the road. She knew she really needed a rain check on this sudden symptom of hers.

Lucy noticed that her mouth was dry as she parked the car, and that her knees were beginning to feel weak.

If she was becoming sick, it was happening quickly. She approached the charming, wrap around porch that surrounded their Victorian-style home as she pulled into their driveway.

She unlocked the door with her keys and went inside. She hurried to the medicine cabinet as soon as she was inside. “Hi, hun," Matt called out. The front of his apron, which he was wearing, was covered in batter.

With the aromas of rosemary, freshly baked bread, and hot honey, the kitchen was heavenly scented.

She felt awful not informing him that she was feeling better because she knew he had been working for hours.

Lucy hastily responded, “Hi baby," before turning to go upstairs to the restroom.

"Are you okay?" Matt questioned her.

As she climbed the steps, she said, "I'll be fine," her voice faltering.

In addition to taking some natural medicines, she also grabbed something from the pharmaceutical cabinet to treat the splitting headache that was starting to develop.

"All right, I'll prepare the table.

It had been ten minutes; Matt made the decision to start alone since he was famished. After 20 minutes, he began to worry and felt the need to check on her.

He heard a loud thud coming from the floor above as he was thinking that. To check on her, he leapt up from his chair.

Matt crossed the kitchen to get to his wife, but as he approached the stairs, the electricity went out, engulfing him in darkness.

Wonderful, he said, adding. In the distance, he could hear the cause of the outage. Thunder, quickly followed by a magnificent lightning flash. Matt fumbled for a torch before dialing his wife.

Matt shouted out to his wife, "Honey."

Zero reaction.

As he entered their bedroom with the flashlight, Matt chuckled to himself. "Baby, doesn't this feel exactly like a scene from a film? Dark home, no power, strange noises coming from up-"

Before Matt could complete his sentence, he overheard coughing and food being spit out into the ground. It's obvious that Lucy has a stomach bug.

Hold on, I'll fetch a towel, I said.

A towel was taken off the shelf in the linen closet in the corridor by Matt. He then went into the bedroom and went straight up to the door of the bathroom.

Matt knocked on the locked bathroom door and yelled, "Baby." "Are you okay?"

Once more, there was silence. When Matt squeaked open the door, a foul odor seeped in and made him gag.

His hands were placed near his nose, while allowing light to enter via the bathroom door's crack.

He felt shivers running down his spine as he opened the door. His wife was there, facing away from him.

In the light of his flashlight, she was naked, and the skin on her almost appeared translucent. Its underside was covered in dark, pulsating veins.

There was a serious problem. As Matt started to retreat, his wife or rather, what was left of her turned around to face him.

Her eyes were a hollow white, lifeless and cold. Matt began to sob and lost his footing as his wife approached him with a snarl.

"Lucy?"

"Lucy, just wait. I'll get you some help." She accelerated toward him like a lion on the hunt for her prey, preventing him from finishing what he was saying. Then Lucy jumped on Matt, he yelled in pain as she dug her teeth into his neck. His body's muscles and blood spattered hers as the blackness started to engulf him.

She was stronger than her husband, who had been coming to the gym every Saturday morning for years, despite her physique having earlier been weak.

Within minutes, she had him in her grasp. She repeatedly bit into him, using her teeth to rip chunks out of his neck that she then swallowed whole.

He screamed in pain at the top of his lungs, until slowly, his voice faded away. His white T-shirt was covered in scarlet, viscous blood, which was also splattered all over the space.

It dripped on the floor in a rhythmic pattern that blended eerily with the sound of the raindrops outside.

The last thing he saw as his life dwindled away were the lifeless eyes of the woman who was supposed to be his wife.

She continued pulling bits of her husband into her mouth even after his body became limp and stopped moving, blood flowing onto the towel her husband had given to her. The window was broken by lightning, which shone light on the bloody chamber.

Chapter 2

*****

The alarm buzzes and wakes Max up, it's a new day. Max recalls the dream he had, Max and Frey grew up listening to stories of the luxurious lifestyle of corysum.

He made a promise to Frey that he would take her to Corysum. But he had lost contact with Frey."

After many years Max has grown up to be a criminal. He’s collaborating with a criminal genius mastermind called Spider.

Spider has formed a rebel operation of more than a hundred people. He wants to illegally get people to Corysum to help people be healed of the diseases that the wealthy had afflicted on them.

Their maniac science operations that they conducted to create new viruses all for their own selfish gain and to make profit from their world power cost Earth a lot.

There was a very costly error in one of the labs, which led to a crazy outbreak of viruses and diseases and mutations.

People were turning into zombies and mutating into monsters. To be fair a couple of rich people who still cared about humanity were funding their research.

To reach Corysum first they needed to acquire a Corysum identification number on their unit which makes them go to any facility on Corysum.

The only way they could get that was from the CEO of Armadyne Cooperation, a bald man called Nigel. He had no compassion for his workers at all.

Max is to work at Armadyne Cooperation to get closer to Nigel. The plan was to kill him to get the identification for Corysum

…….. ……. The Assassination…….

We're running out of time." Max I looked at his wristwatch to confirm what he suspected. It was two minutes passed nine o'clock at night and their target Nigel known for his excessive punctuality was late.

"Relax," Spider said. "If Central said she'll be in her office tonight, she'll be there."

Max peered into the telescopic sight of his sniper rifle. He laid prone on the rooftop of a fifty-floor building with the bipod of his weapon resting on a raised roof edge. Spider laid next to him, tapping the side of a bi-optics binocular.

This was the only position which allowed them to shoot their target without hitting anyone driving avi-cars in the sky.

Through the rifle's scope, He kept his eyes on a luxurious office located twenty-six hundred meters away on the top floor of Eklund & Pride.

The Armadyne company made a fortune from the weapons it produced for Corysum. They also produced drugs that suppressed augmentation sickness.

Anyone who suffered from major injuries to kidney failure needed the latest cyber-tech implant to survive but not everyone was compatible with augmentation.

What happened as a result was illness, and the company liked to leave out the death toll which followed.

It was ironic to Max how Armadyne made the medicine because it was the same company, which created the faulty implants in the first place.

They pretty much made a vaccine to their own virus. He thought it was a little funny how people forgot that. But it wasn't funny when her girlfriend developed symptoms of augmentation sickness.

He remembered when Frey's daughter showed signs of it. The way her hands shook, the odd rhythm of her breathing, the sweating even on cold nights. Then came the worst symptom: darkened blood veins protruding on the skin

They were lucky it wasn't too late when Frey applied for Factor HC1. He remembered the constant, rising bills afterward but it didn’t matter so long as the medicine worked and Frey's daughter got to live longer than the doctor estimated.

Then came the day they were late on payments. Max’s grip on the sniper rifle tightened. All it took was one late payment and the company sent a denial letter rejecting further deliveries of factor.

Now Max laid the hospital, he was on a rooftop ready to murder the one responsible. Of course, it wasn’t all personal, he was also doing this for the good of everyone. They had been deprived of everything; it was only right that he paid for his crimes.

Central informed them the company’s CEO, Nigel, would be in his office for a few minutes tonight to download data for a renewal policy.

This policy will be voted on tomorrow and most likely, it would pass. When it does, the company can withhold factor from anyone regardless of late payments or not.

Spider suspected it was so the company could keep Factor for their wealthier clients even if it meant over three hundred thousand patients will die from augmentation sickness.

The few minutes Nigel would be in his office is the only time to make sure the policy didn't go through and of course to get the identification and data from his DNA to get to Corysum.

Max wasn't going to fail.

"He's here." Spider turned a knob on his binoculars. "Front door."

Spider moved her reticle to the front of the office. Sure enough, there was Nigel and like Central said, she went to her desk to download files.

Spider reported the distance to their target along with the current wind speed and its direction. Max adjusted his aim to make sure he didn't waste a bullet.

One shot, that's all he needed.

But Nigel's son was there and Max couldn't shoot him. Spider tried to convince him that millions of people's lives were at stake if he didn't take the shot but he would have none of it. They left without shooting Nigel, they would have to devise another plan.

Chapter 3

*****

Nigel is having a meeting with some important investors for Corysum and he begins to discuss with them the possibilities of Corysum.

"Corysum is what we call our new utopia that rose from the ashes of a world that was corrupt and scandalous, a world that used money to benefit themselves and let the poor suffer.

Corysum grew from this corrupt society to form a new identity where all the people young and old would live a life that benefits the good of society and not themselves.

Money for us is a thing of the past. Money blinded our ancestors to the point where they become greedy wanting more.

In our new society our currency isn't money but how you can better society through hard work and giving back.

Were a society of inventors, the creators of a world that's free of who we use to be. We're also a society of peace where wars and conflicts are a thing of the past.

The way we resolve conflict is through peaceful mediation. There are times when we get loud but we don't punch and kick each other.

Corysum never seemed like a real possibility generations ago. We fought hard to get to where we are as a people.

We learned from generations of conflicts to create a world where we are free of all the constrains we placed upon ourselves and this new world is the beginning. We're still learning from our past and How we can make our lives even better."

Competition is good in any society. This is how we live a good healthy life, but only if the competition doesn't hurt anyone.

New Earth has good healthy competition. We took sports from the old world and made it into something better, something that we can be proud of.

For example, football in the old world was rough and violent sport that caused untold damage to the body.

We have made football into a non-violent sport that benefits us. I love my job because I get to do two things I love; one is learning about the past.

Two is talking to people, I love when people ask me about how our ancestors lived. What they did wrong and how we can do better.

I gladly answer their questions and they take it all in. What I love most about my job is educating the young. In time they'll be the leaders of New Earth and will be tasked with continuing the legacy we have built.

VR Glasses is common on Corysum. Everyone, the young and old use VR glasses to do normal everyday things like talking to friends and family, sending messages, watching videos, and talking pictures.

The VR glasses works as simple as their name. They're glasses you wear or simply contact lens. They're even easy to use, just put them on and using your Neural Function to turn the glasses on.

Going out buying food at the supermarket or going to restaurants is a thing of the past. We have no use for them anymore, now we have an easy way to make food."

After a couple of minutes of discussion, he shakes hands with them as they leave. Spider is helping 46 humans on Earth to get to Corysum.

The process is very risky as only some who depart make it to Corysum but they're so desperate in spite of the risks at hand.

First they acquire the Corysum identification brands on their wrists. Through the help of Spider, they access three rusty looking spaceships and head for the space station.

As the ships get closer Defense Minister Jessica Dellacourt is alerted about the breach. She contacts Kruger, a rogue agent, and her right-hand man on Earth.

She gives him orders to destroy the spaceships before they can reach Corysum. He follows her orders and fires two air missile launchers on the ships, two of them get shot but one survives. 46 people are killed in the two ships that are destroyed.

Fortunately, the ship lands on Corysum but Jessica gives orders to the Robot Police to stop them.

The Robot Police get to the earthers as they land and many are killed while some are reprimanded. Only a mother and her daughter make it to the med bay.

The mother puts her daughter into the medbay and because of her identification she's healed but in the moment of their joy.

The robots arrest both of them, the earthers who resist are killed while the others are deported back to the Earth.

Chapter 4

*****

After the unfortunate events on Corysum. Two spaceships were destroyed and the casualties of the people was so painful to the society of the Elite called CENTRAL, who supported the Earthers with money for research, and to manage the spaceships. Someone had to be accountable for the damage.

Lieutenant David Phoenix had forgotten how uncomfortable his service uniform was as he made his way through the huge star cruiser to the captain's office.

It was a uniform only for looking nice in and for anal higher ups to nitpick: Dark blue, brass buttons, too-shiny shoes and, to top it all off, a white wheel cap carried beneath his arm.

Over his left breast pocket were the ribbons he had earned and over his right, his surname: Phoenix

He wondered why the ship's captain had called him to his office. Through the winding corridors of the star cruiser Corsair, he made his way passing the various other crew.

Technicians burdened with equipment, mechanics in overalls and grease, marines in full combat gear and rifles.

One room inlaid with steam-burping pipes and wires led to another room where officers were relaxing.

For a man barely over twenty, his face seemed haggard. His dark brown hair was close cropped and his skin pale from being stuck on a ship for a long period of time.

These days his first name sounded foreign to his own tongue. It was always his last name now, or his callsign: Riddler.

Like most pilots he identified with his callsign, it had become his identity now, Davic. Davic was a foolish boy with no home to come back to, now there was only Riddler.

One thing stuck out to Riddler as he continued walking, there seemed to be far less people from when he'd first come aboard.

How long had that been again? He had lost track of time. There was always one more mission to fly one more campaign for Corysum

As his shoes continued clomping on the metallic floors as he wound his way around crewmates, his thoughts had turned to the last mission he had flown with Starfire Squadron:

It was supposed to be a routine patrol around a rocky moon, not a massive fleet battle, not the liberation of a planet. Just a routine patrol.

The Riddler stopped in front of a large window overlooking the vastness of space, barely any stars. The chatter of crew dissolved as his thoughts continued.

Corysum's fighters had jumped them, using the moon's craters to hide from their sensors. Before anyone knew what was happening missiles were being locked onto them.

Flight Leader Zeus gave orders. "Deploy countermeasures! Break off, stay with your wingmen."

The Riddler had barely broken the missile lock and sticking with his wingman Zap. Corysum's fighters were zooming from the moon's surface to meet them.

Riddler got a missile lock and fired, the Corysum fighter deployed countermeasures and opened up with its own guns.

Riddler returned fire. Plasma from both ships impacted shields in a brilliant display until the Sh'ra fighters shields buckled and Riddler's shots went right through the cockpit.

"Splash one!" Riddler called out.

Zap fired a volley of missiles as the Corysum fighter he had been targeting jinked away and deployed countermeasures. One of the missiles managed to find its target, the shields buckled and the craft was sent careening down to the moon it had originally spawned from. But the victory was short lived.

Plasma was already peppering the young humans' shields. The two pilots maneuvered as best they could, but it seemed no matter how they maneuvered some Corysum was on their tail.

“Get this guy off of me!” Riddler shouted, his voice cracking as he feared this was his last flight. As if in answer to his plea the Corysum fighter exploded.

“I'm always having to look out for you hatchlings!” "Thanks for the save, Harpy,” Riddler sighed, grateful for the avian alien.

He continued standing at the window and could almost see the moon and ships fighting and maneuvering around each other now.

The avian didn't reply: There was a burst of static and then nothing, that was the start of things. one by one, the rest of the flight was picked off.

Riddler kept flying and fighting, and by the time he shot down the last fighter. He had a sinking realization that he was all alone in the void, in a damaged ship. Oxygen began leaking out.

Riddler breathed in, glad for the processed, artificial air that now filled his lungs. He saw his reflection in the window and turned away.

If it weren't for his communications equipment still working he never would have made it back to the ship. His mouth was dry as parchment when he finally exited the fighter, his limbs shaking and mind exhausted.

The mechanics all stared at him in bewilderment. Usually, some mechanic would have a clever quip about Riddler damaging their ship, but that day there was only reverent silence.

Riddler was the only survivor of the ambush. After the debriefs, he just sat on his tiny bed in his tiny quarters and stared at the floor.

The men and women he'd fought with for so long were all gone now. He hadn't flown in the days following that incident: not much point in sending a lone pilot out the other squadrons aboard had also taken losses. Riddler wondered what unit of squadron they would put him in

Finally, he arrived at the door of the captain's office as metal gray as everything else on board and was granted permission to enter. The pilot entered and saluted. "Lt. Phoenix reports as ordered Sir!"

The captain was old from years of command: His short snowy white hair contrasting with his dark skin.

His face lined with years of worry carrying the lives of others on his shoulders. The captain returned the salute.

"At ease." Riddler relaxed.

"Do you know why you're here?" The captain asked.

"No, Sir," Riddler replied.

"Care to venture a guess?" The captain asked, leaning back in his gray chair, and resting a file on his lap.

"Is it being the only pilot left in my squadron?"

The captain nodded. "You would be correct." The ship's captain looked ponderous for a bit. "I know it's difficult losing people - especially those you fought with for so long."

"I'm accustomed to loss," Riddler replied.

Frankly," the captain broke in, "I think taking you off flying status and sending you to psych evaluations would be the best thing to do."

Riddler grunted. "Sir, I protest!"

The captain sighed. "You're flying for revenge. I worry it will cloud your judgment: Now that you've lost even more to the enemy, I'm really worried. However, you're still one of our best pilots, and we are short on experienced pilots here lately."

Riddler seemed a bit calmer as he listened.

"We've been ordered to Star base seven for rest, repairs, and resupply. We'll also pick up fresh recruits. With that being said, you're now the flight leader."

Sphinx was taken back to the flight leader. That wasn't his job: Zeus had always been the flight leader.

“I don’t think I’m ready for this responsibility, I’m barely over twenty...”

The captain looked sympathetic. “War doesn’t care. I know it's a lot to put on you, but we don’t have a lot of options.”

You will be very important when we finally have access to the data needed to override corysum's data so consider this an opportunity you must take very seriously.

Chapter 5

*****

The cities of the world were in ruins, with large numbers of zombies and mutant bugs roaming around.

Apart from these monsters, there were also many shelters built by the survivors.

In the morning, the sun's rays shone into fallout shelter 043.

Feeling the sunlight, Max's eyebrows twitched in the room. He opened his eyes and sat up from the bed.

His gaze swept across the room.

As it was doomsday, there was no light, so the room was dark.

Hoo..."

Max exhaled slightly and swept his slightly messy hair.

He got off the bed and came to a shabby calendar in the room.

He tore off a page.

The year 2154, September 12th.

"Doomsday has been going on for more than three years..."

Albert murmured as if he had thought of something that he didn't want to remember.

Three years ago, after a series of science experiments conducted by the Armadyne Corporation for Corysum. A nasty accident by one of the doctors led to the outbreak of the zombie virus

The appearance of zombies quickly caused the world to fall into chaos.

Humans were constantly being killed and eaten.

Within a short week, the crazy zombies had almost engulfed the entire city.

After that, the surviving humans gathered in a block and used cement bags and sandbags to build a line of defense, isolating all the zombies outside.

Ultimately, as the streets continued to be transformed, and weapons, food, and other resources were replenished, they were turned into sanctuaries for the humans during the apocalypse.

Shaking his head and interrupting his memories, Max looked out of the window.

It was early in the morning, and the feeling of an empty stomach from time to time urged him to eat breakfast.

Thinking of this, Max no longer dawdled. He pushed open the door and walked out of the room.

Walking out of the room, he was greeted by the sight of the sanctuary.

It was early in the morning.

As he walked in a familiar direction, Albert also noticed the bustling scene of the people around him.

Because it was doomsday, the living conditions of the people today weren't as good as before.

Most of the people around him didn't wear shoes, and their clothes were tattered.

They were all focused on their own matters.

But when walking past them, these people would always turn their eyes to look at Max and greet him with a smile.

Max looked outside at what was left of their home and he remembered his parents once again and the events that changed everything. It changed him for life.

It was a bank robbery, he wanted to go to an amusement park with his parents. They had to stop in a bank to get some cash. Though their luck was pretty bad because at that time there was a robbery going on in that bank.

When the thief demanded money from the cashier, Max's dad picked up a shattered glass piece which dropped to the ground while the thief was shooting to a random place and try to get the attention of everyone.

Max's dad stabbed the thief on the neck

and when blood gushed out like a fountain a gunshot heard by everyone. There was another thief in the crowd, he was disguised as a civilian with sweat and jeans.

He panicked when he saw Max's dad approaching to his companion and shot randomly to Max's dad. He was aiming for his leg but his hand was shaking due to extreme amount of anxiety.

His aim got distorted and shot Max's dad on the heart. Other thief was dead but it wasn't important to Max. He saw his father getting shot and was powerless to stop it.

Max started running to the man which shot his father and jumped on him. The other thief was shaking because of taking a human life and he wasn't in the right mindset to dodge Max

He started to punch the thief with his little hands. After getting a punch the thief came to himself and he lifted Max with all of his power and throw him to a hard wall. His mother was watching all of the events happening in front of her with teary eyes.

Max's mother saw that the thief was aiming towards Max with his gun so she got in front of Haru. Another gunshot heard by everyone in the bank.

Haru's mother saw that the thief was aiming towards Haru with his gun so she got in front of Max. Another gunshot heard by everyone in the bank.

Max looked at his mother's corpse while the thief was running towards the exit. He didn't mind that though he just looked straight into his mother's eye.

"Hey Max, don't cry, it is not a problem, I'll be okay. “Said his mother with a low voice.

"No mom please don’t leave me, I need you. “Ax said while pressing the wound on his mother's abdomen she was losing so much blood. running towards the exit.

He didn't mind that though he just looked straight into his mother's eye. "Hey Max, don't cry, it’s not a problem, I'll be okay. “Said his mother with a low voice.

"No mom please don’t leave me, I need you. “Ax said while pressing the wound on his mother's abdomen she was losing so much blood.

Max cried that day for the last time until officers came. Since that day he has trained to use guns and weapons of all kinds. He developed a strong connection with the sniper and it became his signature weapon.

He became a renowned criminal; a professional hitman and he got great satisfaction in sniping those that killed his parents.

With the apocalypse on Earth, he joined the rebels in the fight against the zombies and the mission to make the Earthers a citizen of Corysum.

Chapter 6

*****

When Spider informed Max and Jugo about the operation he thought he was crazy. He told them they were basically living in a program, a contest against the Albadyne company so this is some form of Matrix shit.

Spider was like their bodies would be in the lab, they would be implanted with some chips into them they got from the CEO of Albadyne.

The whole thing was bizarre but they had to do this to save thousands of people and stage the rebellion.

Unsurprisingly, the explosion was vast and all consuming. One spark ignited an unattended gas leak, triggering a military storage of chemical weapons to fulminate. It incinerated everything within a mile radius and killed thousands.

To those unlucky enough to witness the plant's catastrophic failure, it would be a tragedy seared forever in their memories.

For Max, it was infuriating.

"If that lanky prick bumps into me one more time I'm going to decapitate him." He pulled out a chrome tallier, its white-on-black digits read 0087. He clicked the trigger. A bright flash engulfed him.

From the safety of the observatory respawn, he was back in the main hall. His stubby comrade, Jugo, was sitting on a couch with a cocky grin. He stood up.

“You know, you were so close that time, really. If it wasn’t for the one boney soldier-”

“I’m going to decapitate him.” Jeremy huffed before he could finish.

“Yes. That would look amazing on the rankings, bud.”

Of course, causing any harm or being captured to any course civilians was a score deduction. To lead the ranks, you couldn’t get caught. Next to agility and improvisation, stealth was the hardest challenge in the history lobbies.

Mike saw his friend was close to quitting, he relented.

“Hey, let’s take a breather, let's grab a drink before the next round.” He patted Jeremy on the shoulder, who took a deep breath and sighed.

"Fine!"

The two walked through the crowd of other players in the main hall, succeeding and struggling in their own courses. Three women were arguing loudly outside the Halifax room, likely arguing strategies. Some kid and his friends left the Vesuvius lobby in hysterics, covered in dust. It was popular with birthday parties.

Oh, all the courses in the Disaster Hub, there was no greater challenge than the Redstone Incident of 2027. The end was anti-climactic, all you had to do was turn off a gas line to stop the explosion.

It was managing to navigate an entire military complex in sixty minutes without being captured or shot by military police that was the challenge. Only three people were able to finish since its debut. None of them shared how they did it.

Satisfied with their sodas, the two sat and stewed. In the past couple years, the two have been able to win every history course.

Hiroshima, Halifax, New York, Chernobyl, even the Waco room before it was discontinued. They'd always found a way to win all of them. All except Redstone.

"The starting point is way too conspicuous," Jeremy bemoaned between sips. "I mean I'm supposed to just appear at the front doors of an armory?"

Mike countered, "It's definitely not like they have heavy guards in the lobby or anything. It's just Carol."

He half-snickered, "She's a sweetheart." Jeremy leaned back in his chair, hands cupping his face. He rubbed his temples.

> "Okay," he started, "We can't access the labs without entering through the front. We can't just run past or the alarms go off."

"You can't hit the dead end on the left, either. Plus, there's only one stairwell to the lower level." Mike lamented. "Seems no matter where you walk around you're going to raise suspicion." He sipped more cola.

Jugo sat back up, still puzzled. He backtracked.

"We only have three inventory items."

"Allen wrench, glowstick, and the key card to the testing room. Yup."

"The access key, I get. But what the hell are the screwdriver and glow stick for?"

"Honestly," Max recalled, "Maybe the Allen wrench turns off the gas line?"

"And the glow stick?"

Max looked up, cocking an eyebrow. He took a sip before guessing, "to celebrate?"

The two finished gulped the last of their drinks and stood up. They cleared their table and made their way back to the Redstone room. An older muscular guy was leaving as they were approaching, a familiar look of frustration plastered on his face.

The pair entered the lobby. Jeremy placed his tallier on the loading pad.

"Player JEREMY BANE. Attempt number EIGHTY-EIGHT. Please click-in when you're ready."

Both of them took communication buds and placed them in their ears. Jeremy grabbed the tallier, along with the inventory pack, securing it around his waist. Then stepped into the transport zone.

The game clock above his head reset to a bright red 60:00. He looked back to his friend and held up a tight fist.

"Eighty-eighth times the charm, right?"

"It better be" Max hit his fist.

With a click, Jugo was back at the facility doors. Yet again, he only had an hour to turn off the gas line and prevent disaster.

Failure meant the deaths of thousands of innocent civilians, not to mention an even more battered ego.

He pushed open the glass doors into the sterile beige armory. An older, blonde woman in professional attire sat behind a tidy desk, tapping away at a computer.

"Hello there, what are you here for Sir?"

"No time, Carol." Jugo replied. "Where's the nearest bathroom?"

Carol was confused. However, she cautiously pointed to her left. "Uh...just down that small hallway, second door on the left."

"Thanks."

He marched hurriedly down the hall to the men's room; his ear began to chatter with Max's own confusion.

"What are you doing, there's no time for this! Get your ass downstairs."

As he approached the urinal, Jeremy retorted "Well whose idea was it to gulp down a large soda?"

Max, ignoring the accusation, just replied "Hurry. Up."

Finished, Jugo zipped up. He figured he would just try outrunning Military Police and see how well that would go this time.

He walked over the mirror to rinse his hands off first, not wanting to catch some century-old virus.

He noticed something in the mirror, above one of the stalls was a large metal vent. A vent with four hexagonal screws.

Unzipping the inventory pack around his waist, he fished out the Allen wrench.

"No way."

He opened the stall and stood on the yellow-stained toilet. Fortunately, he was tall enough to reach each screw. They wrench fit perfectly.

"No way." Max parroted the same amazed disbelief back.

"Max, if we beat this course because of a pee break, we have to come up with a better story to tell everyone."

He began to work at the screws. In a few minutes, the fourth was nearly off. Slowly, he balanced the loose vent cover and gently placed it down in the stall below.

“This is going to suck," Jugo complained.

Between the toilet’s exposed pipes, the top of the stalls, and the vent’s opening, Jeremy had to hoist himself up without raising alarms or breaking his neck.

Balancing one foot on the toilet and another wedged against the stall, he had just enough reach for one forearm to hook into the air duct and his other hand on its edge.

Just as he lifted in, a knock came from the door.

“Sir. Sir, are you okay?” Carol called from the other side.

“Oh no.” Jugo said under his breath.

He yelled back, dangling from the waist. “Uh, yes Ma’am, just not feeling well.”

“Oh,” she continued, noticeably concerned “well my apologies. I can tell whoever you’re here to see you’re indisposed, if you like.”

“Damn it, Carol, why do you have to be so attentive,” Max chirped to his friend.

“N-no ma’am,” Jeremy called back to her, ignoring the joke. “I think I’ll just…finish up and come back tomorrow. Don’t want to get him sick.”

With shaking arms and building sweat, Jugo lifted the rest of his body up before he lost his strength.

“Okay well, sorry to bother you, Sir. I’ll come back and check on you in a bit, though. Don’t want anybody dying on me," she said, then walked away with an awkward chuckle. Jeremy sighed in relief.

He reached back into his inventory pack again, grabbed the emerald glow stick and cracked it. In seconds, neon light flooded the frigid maze. Now he just needed directions.

"Alright, I'm up here…Now what. I don't exactly have a map."

There was a pause on the other side. "Well," Max finally responded, "if the lab is in the lower level, you can start with a way down. And you've got forty-one minutes to find it."

Jugo set off down the metal prism, mindfully crawling on his stomach. It was as cold as expected, yet strangely calm.

What was an anticipated rush of chilled air was more of a light breeze humming against his ears. Besides the hum, there was only the sporadic clang of arms and legs trying not to be heard below.

After a couple minutes came the first fork in the ducts. Without any kind of blueprints for the ac system, any way could be as good as any.

However, based on eighty-seven other errors, the best chance was right. The only open stairwell on the first floor ran down the building's east wing.

As Jugo started down the right side, he was startled by muffled sirens that blared in the rooms below him.

"I guess Carol checked on me after all," he reported to Max

"Told you, she's a sweetheart."

With no further care for preventing alarms, Jugo dropped all ease of pace. He clattered down the duct until he found what seemed like a dead end.

After a few feet, it revealed to be quite the opposite. It was a cool aluminum slide to the basement floor.

The only problem is that it was completely vertical, there was no room to turn feet-first.

Stuck in place, Jugo wiped frigid sweat from his face. In the midst of claustrophobia, rolling alarms, and a rotation of marching patrol in the halls below, there was no other option.

He had to dive down and hope he wouldn't crack his skull. He began to turn on his back and asked for an update from his partner.

"Twenty-nine minutes left," Max reported bluntly.

"Great."

Now upside down, Jugo scooted forward. As his head hung over the edge, he pressed his palms against the smooth walls of the downward duct.

Slowly, he worked his way over the edge, arching his back to a near breaking point. Once the edge was at his waste, he stretched his right knee to the same wall. Then the left. With every muscle in his body, he managed to fully hold himself facing what was now a five-foot drop.

He began to crawl inch by inch, one appendage at a time. All his force was pressing his back against the wall as he struggled to hold himself. Sweat collected on every limb, then began dropping below. His eyes stung; the walls were lubricated with four feet still to go.

He first lost grip with his right palm with three feet left to go. He darted back, shaking the entire duct. Reverberation flooded his ears.

"No, no, no, no, no," Jugo panicked. He couldn't get situated properly. He fell straight down, two and a half feet.

He smacked the metal directly below. Unintentionally, he managed to avoid breaking his neck when he slid in the slick of his own sweat. Broken and drained, he stayed down at the start of the basement duct. For a minute, the only sounds were random pained groans.

“Jugo! Are you with me man?” Mike panicked, trying to get him to move. “Should hit the return pad?”

Jugo thought about it, every part of his body was in pain. His tooth was chipped, he was half-sure his left elbow imploded.

But he was at the basement level, just down the hall from glory.

“I’ll sue the company later, we gotta win this. Time.”

Max checked the game time. “Nineteen minutes.”

It was a great time. Only now they were flying blind. Even worse, Jugo's only glow stick broke in half, splattering the ducts and himself in a horror show of grassy pulp. He pressed on.

"So, what do I do now? Is there any hint at which direction the lab is in?"

Max was silent yet again on the other end. "I'm sorry man. For once, I've got nothing to say. This stinks."

Jugo labored forward. In front was a dark dead end. As he approached, he discovered two new hopes.

There was a perpendicular duct that ran left and an increasing need to vomit. The air ducts flooded with the stench of rotten eggs.

"The gas leak…" Jugo pieced the history together. "We're winning this."

With a vanishing green tint, he floundered down the rancid tube. With every passing grate, he inhaled deep.

Until, on a seventh whiff, he nearly puked. There was a faint hiss in the room attached, barely audible among the faint sirens of the facility above.

Frantically, he started smashing an elbow against the grate. There was no time or room for tools, time was running down.

“How Much Time Left, he ordered between slamming’s.

“Four minutes! Get in there!”

Eventually, the grate bent out and the screws came loose. The grate fell to the floor in a clatter. Jugo inched forward, then backed up his feet as carefully as he could through the great. When he reached his waist, he pushed. He slammed to the tile below on his back.

"Please take me to a doctor after this," He pleaded to his friend.

Managing to stand, he worked his way to a light switch and flipped it. He surveyed the room for the source of hissing. Every Bunsen burner had a red handle, only one of them was facing up.

Jugo staggered to the burner; he slammed it down. The hissing stopped; Max cheered in his ear, they won.

He fished out the chrome tallier. The white-on-black digits read 0088, he clicked the trigger. A bright flash engulfed him.

Max started waking up, and the first thing he remembered was that my head hurt.

At lot.

Everything was black except for the dim lights that were overhead. I wouldn't call them lights, in the same sense as fluorescent lights. It was more a glow, like the glow that you would get from a glow stick that one would use in the wilderness at night.

They were very high up - 30 feet or more. And there was a slight vibration in the floor. I could tell that I was inside some sort of vehicle.

It was massive.

He tried to get up, but as he rose to his feet, his head swam, and immediately dropped to my knees. He was still very week, he wanted to walk around to get a feel for my surroundings.

The next best thing was to just sit down and take a look around me.

He looked to his immediate left and he noticed a girl who was lying down in a medical-like cot about 10 feet away from me.

She seemed to be sleeping, but she was making a strange gurgling noise that didn't sound like snoring.

She was vomiting.

He immediately rushed over to her. She already seemed to be choking and was jerking and convulsing in its failing attempts to keep the liquid out of her lungs.

I immediately turned her over on her side. I sat on the cot and held her body on its side as I tried to get her vomit from hitting the floor without falling to the bed. As I wiped her mouth I was able to notice that she was breathing.

At least that was a good sign.

But she was still asleep, sedated, knocked out, or whatever that had happened to the both of us.

But before I had the chance to concentrate my thoughts and efforts into pondering what exactly had brought the two of us there.

I became immediately distracted by what I saw around us. We weren't only the only people there. In the dim of the light, I could see other bodies, either completely still or barely moving.

there were thousands.

Suddenly, very large holograms seemed to spring up out of the floor. Each one was an image an image of a 3D cartoon face.

They had bright smiles, they were large - at least 10 feet tall. The holograms were evenly spaced about 20 feet apart and seemed to extend down what appeared to be an endless hallway.

A loud alarm started blaring. It sounded like something you would hear if you won something at a casino.

" Attention contestants! Attention contestants! "

The voice was very positive and playful.

"Congratulations on your selection. My name is BiBi, your friendly game moderator. We have a lot of information to cover and very little time. Please wake from your sleep and direct your attention to the coordinator when he speaks."

“Who was the coordinator?”

As all of this was happening, there was an increase of activity inside whatever moving structure we were in.

What used to be a sea of almost motionless silhouettes was beginning to resemble a crowd of active human beings.

People were rising to their feet and those too weak and disoriented to do so were sitting up in their cots.

Almost as soon as the game moderator was done speaking, a large flat screen began to rise out of the floor next to each hologram.

The screens were twice as large as the game moderator. BiBi turned "her" attention to the screen as if long-awaited but very exciting information was about to be announced by someone very important.

The murmuring of the thousands present seemed to subside on its own.

The black screens flickered to life. There was a man in a black suit sitting on a large red leather chair.

Judging be the shelves upon shelves of books that were behind him, he seemed to be inside of an elegant study or library. He was wearing a cat mask that came from a different time period and was oriental in nature.

After about a few seconds of silence, he began to speak.

"Greetings contestants. My name is Belisarius. I am the coordinator. I wish to welcome you to a very grand endeavor, to which all of us are now apart. You may not know it yet, but all of you participants in a historical moment."

Everyone's eyes were glued to the screen.

"War has been instrumental in moving mankind forward. It's what brought us out of caves, and into the leviathan cities that we live in under the waves.

But before the majority of our planet was covered in water, there were different countries, borders, religions, and creeds.

We refer to these times as the “barbaric ages” when man was constantly at war. He perfected this art to the point where our species was brought to the brink of extinction."

"We know live in the "achievement age.” We live under the waves in our mega cites, the kind that mankind has never seen, and we have world peace.

But this has led to an unexpected problem. Without war, or any form of conflict whatsoever, humanity has become stagnant and progress has all but disappeared. Upon seeing this I was forced to ask myself: '

“What’s worse?”

“Stagnation or destruction?”

I’ll tell you that they are one in the same. Stagnation is just assured destruction in slow motion."

"Now that I have confessed my thoughts to all of you regarding the predicament that both myself and all of you are in, I'm sure you're asking yourself:

"What does he plan on doing about it?"

"That's what brings us to our present situation. Currently, all of you listening to my voice are on the General Brusilov air carrier, flying 20,000 feet above the earth's surface.

For all of you, this is your first time leaving the sanctuaries below the ocean that have been the cradle of human civilization for the past 700 years. What likely none of you know, is that approximately 100 years ago, the ocean began to recede."

As he was talking, a map of the earth was shown on the screen, and it zoomed in on areas of land that I had never seen before nor new existed.

"About a decade ago, a country known in the pre-modern era as Vietnam, became habitable again. During the last phase of the barbaric ages, there was a conflict between the great nations of the world known as the Vietnam War.

During that war there was a battle known as Khe Sanh. 80,000 soldiers, men and women fought for a small strip of land over a period of months.

Their widely differentiating beliefs on how humanity should live on this earth caused them to do everything in their power to kill those on the opposite side of this miniscule piece of land."

"This is what all of you will dd, this is why you all are here."

"You'll be repeating this battle, everyone in this air ship is on one side. There's another ship headed to the same location, you'll use the same ancient tactics and technology of those days to fight for victory.

In order to survive, you must come together as a united army. You'll be given the role of an ancient country of North Vietnam and her allies in the field.

The other 40,000 opponents, your enemies, will play the role of an ancient Empire known as the United States of America. "

"You'll take part in a battle of dominance, a clash of civilizations and ideologies."

"I'm sure you are wondering why you should participate in this affair: This reenactment. This game if you will, because after all, you do have a choice to participate or not."

"First of all, I'd like to bring your attention to the collars around your neck."

I put my hands to my neck and I noticed there was a collar. I tried to take it off, but it wouldn't budge.

"You can't take these collars off. They have a timer, and once it detonates, there's a small explosive that will kill you.

But if you're victorious in this battle, the collars will be deactivated. If you win, you and all who have survived will have full and uninhibited dominion of all the land that you have fought on."

"This is my solution to the crisis that humanity is currently in." Now that I have explained everything, I have just one question for you.

"Will you play?"

"We join me for the sake of humanity."

"What's your answer?"

The screen went black, and there was nothing more.

www.ingramcontent.com/pod-product-compliance
Lightning Source LLC
LaVergne TN
LVHW052053160826
845678LV00015B/3195

9798353220671